The Geometry of Purpose

Everything was created for a purpose.

Craig Gomes

Ukiyoto Publishing

What's the music of the Universe? It's a collection of sounds and activity created by everything unfolding around it, all the time, at levels you can hear and also at levels you cannot - an interwoven fabric. It never stops. Neither do you. You continue to unfold and grow more and more into yourself.

You are an essential part of the fabric of this Universe. Just as you move through the Universe, it moves through you, interwoven into a fabric. Sound is only one dimension of this fabric. Just as sound waves move through ears and make the inner self vibrate and resonate to create signals and value for the one who listens, you move through the music of the Universe, resonating and creating value as well. Everything in this universe was created on purpose, for a purpose.

Contents

Chapter 1

Into The Unknown

The universe is approximately 13.8 billion years old, while the earliest humankind only first appeared a few million years ago on this tiny insignificant speck of dust, in an ever-expanding and never-ending universe which is, in turn, moving towards its own life. As time passed, humankind evolved. We created fire, carved inscriptions on stone and even built the wheel. The evolution of humankind brought with it advances in science, technology, and innovation. Despite the continuous evolution of human beings, science, technology, and philosophy in this relatively short existence of ours, we began asking too many questions that we have failed to answer yet.

We have always wanted to know and understand our role in this universe. We wanted to know our purpose, a solution for our existential crisis. This paved the way for belief systems, theories directed to answers to our biggest questions. Religion has been trying to explain the existence of everything for years. While a large number of us have accepted it, there are several things that religion too could never answer. According to the religious theory, humans are at the center of everything and they are a level below the creator who is watching over everything that he created. While the theory of religion has been satisfactory for most, to this day, many of us even dedicate our entire lives in the search for truth. We all take different paths in life. While we humans continuously evolve and still struggle with the same questions as before: "Who are we? What are we doing here? What is life? What is all this around me? Why am I, myself?"

As time passed, each day and night, spread confusion amongst human beings about their existence. Our world has become a place where we are trying to draw order by the use of chaos, we are proposing alternate realities, we are discussing new ideas, we humans trying to live in harmony with everything around us which contradicts everything because of our very nature, because in reality we are only trying to end the life of our only home, this planet we live in.

Being in such a world, I have been thinking a lot about this and I have an idea I want to propose. The idea is very easy to go through and is fun to speak about. They may or may not make sense but at least I think I will be delivering a point. These thoughts also have their origin in the brain of an evolved human. My brain thinks that these ideas are worth being discussed and so, let's do it.

After reading Douglas Adams's "The Hitchhiker's Guide to The Galaxy", I thought about his ideas a lot. Let's imagine this world to be a computer and us humans as part of the computer. What if we are just tiny, next to useless parts of a machine in a smaller computer (earth) in a large expansive universe? Maybe other universes exist too, who knows? I think that slightly changes our perception of being created by an almighty being who is always watching us and our lives are not a rehearsal.

Well, here are my arguments. Evolution goes first. We all know that humans have evolved and we should know that computers have evolved as well. Remember history, when the fire was first invented, then came the wheel; it has been a long journey since then, and here we are today. Great civilizations have risen and fallen, there was a renaissance and there probably will be another, who knows? We have emerged as explorers and are traveling from our planet to the moon and Mars and we might soon get to know everything about this universe and beyond.

People have been studying the science of objects and viewing it from different perspectives and making some breakthroughs day in and day out. With the experience we have in this universe we can comfortably say that any child born today can think that the life expectancy is up to 79 years yet we do not even have a solution to climate change. It is evident that as humans we have evolved and are still evolving. Likewise, quantum computers are an evolved successor to the classical computer. They may differ in functions just like no human is communicating through smoke signals or writing on leaves anymore.

As humans, we have evolved from hunting for survival to hunting for leisure to being against animal hunting and here we are talking about animal husbandry being a threat to the climate. There has been an ascending gradient starting from the era when Alan Turing invented the original machine a few decades ago and in the present quantum computers. Just like the original revolutionary machine by Alan Turing, quantum computers are also revolutionary and this has happened in only a century.

There will be a time when everything will be optimized and a new version of computers will arise which will perform different tasks just like the evolution of humankind. Classical computers were binary and they could process so much but they had a limited number of pathways for thought processes. Yes, and no were the only options in existence and for each option, there was a separate transistor. Quantum computers are now in existence and since they have properties of a continuous spin, superposition and entanglement, it is expected that they will answer questions that we even do not have, including those which we have pondered for all of humanity's existence. Quantum computers will make hypotheses and formulate questions at a much higher level of permutation and combination that we can fathom using quantum properties.

Let's think about this analogically? The earth in itself is a computer that has kept in itself a very stable environment and as humans, we are the computing and processing units and the software of the computer that utilizes the surrounding as hardware and external support to optimize our outputs. We have built computers and have given names to processes like machine learning or artificial intelligence.

Has it ever crossed your mind that we are structured in a way that is more advanced than the computers we have built today? Would there be more and better progress if the entire computer (world) worked as one instead of each one of us trying to find our cause and the entire computer works towards a single cause? I think there would. What about you? Maybe a point in life will come when we will realize that we were created millions of years ago and stored in this universe by far more advanced ways than the computers we are creating.

The hardware and software of a computer need a stimulating and relaxed environment to function. Likewise, quantum computers should be stored in a stable environment to keep them working properly. The solar system and the entire galaxy too need such an environment. We might be convinced to think that they only require the internal system for them to be stable. In humans, the software is running in our brains and implemented on the surroundings we live in and later use the ecosystem around us to optimize the results.

Oxygen, a natural resource around us, is used for us to perform more efficiently. Likewise, in a computer, the type of processing units present determine the computer's efficiency and we are the ones who create the optimal conditions for it. The way we use resources from our surroundings to optimize our lives may be helping us in giving the required output. There might be chances that the climate changes and burden we are putting on this planet were an inevitable aspect like the deterioration of batteries over time and use.

When the batteries deteriorate, we replace them with others. What if it occurs, that when the inevitable aspects on this planet show up, we move to some other place like Mars or some other planet and then move out when required? Maybe the entire universe is a collection of computers that is regulated from the outside and that is why there is continuous expansion. Maybe there are a different set of properties outside the universe that help in governing the system and those properties are responsible for the universe to come into existence.

Very close to evolution is survival of the fittest. By this, we mean that the better genes are retained and passed through the test of time while the bad ones are omitted or deleted. Our programs or software are continuously debugged to ward off mistakes that might render the program inefficient or even useless. Mutation can also use this principle. One who wants to further this theory of such a system could go ahead to say that just like transistors of a computer alternate between 0 and 1, we switch on and off. On is getting up and off is sleeping. Besides, like quantum superposition during the spin, we live carrying out activities, dreaming, get into comas and live in vegetative states or even die.

When measured, we read only one of the two, either awake or asleep or dead and alive. With the natural course and with our circadian rhythms given, while half the world is awake, the other half is asleep. However, when stuck between problems, we reject sleep and food until we get over the bump or give in and give up. We are always in the system, working one way or another just to keep it running. In this system, we can view each person having a different function.

We could be serving a different purpose to maintain the internal sustainability of the system to keep it from collapsing. In his book, Douglas Adam says that the computer earth was built to answer the greatest question of living beings: life, the universe, which is generally everything. This can mean that it was built to help us understand what is happening around us, to answer why we live and the purpose of life. We are helping someone out there to achieve what we think we can achieve by advancing quantum computers.

Based on all this, we can conclude that the main purpose of our lives is to find a purpose. However, this purpose is not for ourselves but someone else. By doing what we do, living, we are helping another person achieve what we are hoping to achieve with the advancement of the quantum computer for starters. The lives we live are helping another person achieve their main goal or their target. Many altruistic humans who live on this planet might concur with me when it comes to this theory. Most would agree to this. The theory means we spend all our life helping another person achieve what they want in life, helping another population of beings to achieve its course.

Should we, homo sapiens, the primitive beings come to extinction to pave way for a new version of human beings who are superior to us: artificial intelligence? When you get yourself thinking about this theory, many questions will come to mind. This theory says that we are insignificant parts of a certain computer. Does this mean that being inside a computer as its inner parts, we are additionally trying to build computers within the larger mentioned computer? Are we trying to recreate life on earth in a better way by creating computers inside a computer?

If yes, do the existing human beings need to be extinct to pave the way for the new superior race with advanced artificial intelligence? We as human beings are considered the force of nature and maybe this in itself classifies as a course of evolution just like the rest. The secrets and reasons for our existence and that of the universe are discovered where it is least expected. We discover all this as we try to make and invent new things. It is through the inventions that we discover the reason why we are living and where we came from.

Has it ever crossed our minds that one day these computers which we are building might become human? This clearly explains the statement, a life that we usually find the reasons and explanations of our existence in the inventions we make. As each day passes by, you find humans putting their brains together to make something that has never been in existence, they want to make an invention. There are chances that after the invention is done, we might relate our existence and that of the universe to that which has been invented.

Maybe those who were inventing computers were not trying to make them have similar qualities as those possessed by human beings. Instead, as they are making and advancing the computers in technology, it is then that they realize that we are made just like computers and we have qualities present in computers, we are just building what we are in the computers but not copying our qualities into them.

I think that when such topics are brought up, people should participate fully and bring out their views and opinions. In the past centuries and decades, technology and development came to existence and after a short while topics of discussion came up. Our minds have not been constantly engaged to think about such things and have not been working at their full capacity and this now needs to show up. I think a renaissance could help, as it would revolutionize this planet of ours.

We should not just sit and watch everything happening. There is a rise in development and after people toured the moon almost half a century ago, no further efforts have been made. Humanity needs to move forward and it is us who will see to it that it moves forward. Sitting still in a moving vehicle taking us forward in space will not help us in making humanity move forward. I think it is high time that people speak out their ideas without fear of criticism or anything. People out there have great thoughts but you are not helping anyone when you keep the thoughts to yourself. Speak out and let's see whether we can make your thoughts a reality, maybe you have a solution on how we can move to Mars or another planet.

I believe most of us believe that everything is symmetrical and binary. Since the existence of quantum computers, we nowadays accept superposition and entanglement. The way we think and our capacities have also evolved in almost a similar way of the same. A good example is that of gender; gender was binary then but look at us now, we are on a non-binary path. Evolution makes everything whole. Small things like gender to bigger things like innovation are all based on our thinking processes.

We have allowed our brains to be open to things that are not symmetrical. We have also allowed our brains to understand and apply the laws of quantum physics. Maybe this is the main reason why we do not perceive other dimensions which might be the solutions to our evolution questions.

It is clear by now that we cannot explain such facts nor can we determine them. All we need to do is understand what is most important of us humans and acknowledge our limitations. We should also understand that just because something is accepted by many people it is not necessarily right.

Chapter 2

The Vanishing Point

Have you ever pondered the limits of your vision? Contemplating the universe's origins, its intricate history, and its current state can be a mind-bending journey. The theory of the Big Bang suggests that the universe burst into existence approximately 13.8 billion years ago. It was then that the universe was born, brimming with matter and radiant energy, fostering the formation of stars, galaxies, planets, and eventually, life itself. But how far can we truly see? Conventional wisdom dictates that, given the age of the universe and the constant speed of light, our vision extends roughly 13.8 billion light-years in every direction. Yet, this figure merely scratches the surface of the cosmos' true expanse. In reality, our gaze penetrates a staggering 46 billion light-years in all directions, encompassing a vast diameter of 92 billion light-years. This raises a profound question: why this boundless reach? Exploring this enigma unveils three intuitive perspectives, each offering a unique lens through which to perceive the cosmos. However, only one of these perspectives aligns with reality, inviting us to delve deeper into the mysteries that shroud our understanding of the universe.

Light travels at the speed of light, and there is an object in every different place.

This is actually what most of us think to be the right way to describe this situation. Imagine a universe that is full of stars and galaxies everywhere a person looks, and these stars and galaxies began forming long before anything else was formed. By this, it can easily be understood that the longer we wait, the further we can see, since light travels in a straight line at the speed of light. The world is currently 13.8 billion years old; we expect to see back around 13.8 billion light-years and then subtract from that to know how long it took for the stars and galaxies to form after the Big Bang.

Light moves at the speed of light (c), and everything can move through space, with an object in every different place.

This perspective adds another layer of complexity to the understanding of the universe. There is a plethora of objects emitting light, and these objects can also move relative to one another. According to the rules of special relativity, these objects can move at speeds approaching the speed of light, although not necessarily at the same velocity. Consider a scenario where light moves in your direction at the speed of light. In this case, you would perceive objects as being twice as far away compared to the previous scenario. Therefore, if we assume that the light has just reached us and that the objects are moving away from us at almost the speed of light, they would now be approximately 27.6 billion light-years away.

Light travels at the speed of light (c), while stars and galaxies are in constant motion. Additionally, the universe is expanding, and there is an object in every different place.

This perspective presents the most challenging aspect for people to grasp. Space, as we understand it, is teeming with matter that coalesces into stars, galaxies, and even larger structures with remarkable speed. The light emitted by these celestial bodies moves through space at the speed of light in a vacuum, denoted as c. The mutual gravitational attraction between different regions of varying densities facilitates the movement of matter throughout space.

Probably something that very few of us know is that space itself is expanding. Have you ever looked at a distant galaxy and realized that it is redder than normal? If yes, have you ever wondered why that happens? We might think that it is red because it is moving far away from us and the wavelength becomes longer, hence redder, just like the way a siren, which is moving away from our direction, has its sound shifted to longer wavelengths and lower pitches. Is that the only explanation?

In addition to that, general relativity adds the extra element of space expanding. As the universe expands due to relativity, the fabric of space also stretches, making the individual light waves in that particular space stretch their wavelengths. It might be thought that these two effects cannot be told apart. As a person who measures light wavelength as it reaches your eye, can you tell whether it is happening due to motion or due to the fabric of space? As shown, there is a visible relationship that exists between the redshift and therefore the wavelength and the observed brightness of the galaxy which is normally a function of distance.

In a universe that is not expanding, as earlier seen, the maximum distance that we can see is twice the age of the universe in light-years, in this case, 27.6 billion light-years. This cannot be used today since we have seen galaxies at a larger distance than that. What do you think you can see in any direction? If the universe contained only bright energy and no dark energy, all the furthest objects, which include the stars, galaxies, and leftover glow from the Big Bang, would be limited to 41.4 billion light-years. In a universe with dark energy, like ours, that gets pushed to a larger number: 46 billion light-years for the observed dark energy possessed by our cosmos.

When all that is put together, the distance we can see in the universe from one distant end to the other is 92 billion light-years across. The expansion of the universe and the presence of dark energy have led to 97% of the observable world being unreachable.

We should realize that space itself is expanding and new space is getting created in between the bound galaxies, groups, and cosmos. Due to this, the universe looks so big in our eyes. Based on what is in the universe, how it came to be, and what governs it, no other way would have come out. Most folks at one point or another have detected something concerning panpsychism, which is the theory that the complete universe is acutely aware. This has been existing in several forms across the centuries and in many various cultural and spiritual settings. Plato, the traditional thinker, believed in one thing known as the "World-Soul". A god variety within the Hindus believed that the universe was a living illusion from a god. Plenty of neopagans believe that the world features are acutely aware of the spirit "Gaia". As Christians too, we tend to be unseen since we tend to conjointly evoke the thought of the pervasive "Holy Spirit".

Being spiritual or not, there are high possibilities that the arguments below can cause you to have a brand-new perspective on this planet.

Integrated scientific theory

Most folks can agree that consciousness could be a strange development. Occasionally scientists notice it when handling consciousness only that it's next to not possible to induce it from initial principles or, perhaps in a better language, it's not extremely contributing to the subtractive method of recent science. The elemental elements of the brain together with the neurons and atoms don't have anything that once was supplementary. All along they have been compelled to generate the phenomenological expertise of consciousness like the expertise of color red or the subjective feeling of joy. These are things that philosophers ask as "qualia" and this has been known as the "hard downside of consciousness".

Therefore, rather than functioning from the bottom up, brain doctor Giulio Tononi projected a top-down approach called Integrated scientific theory. The idea says that we will classify consciousness in terms of the common factors shared by all the items we all know have consciousness. Out of these, Tononi says that all of them have some common properties: they collect information and that they integrate it. This theory proposes a definition of consciousness because of the integration of knowledge. This theory, just like any complicated system is often an allotted variety that tells you ways in which that integrated system is. The quantity gives you an information-theoretical life of consciousness. Any system that has been allotted variety bigger than zero has a point of consciousness.

Let's visit one thing that is a little bit strange. It's nearly obvious that this definition includes animals and humans with brains. I hope we have understood up to this point. However, it conjointly includes machines. This still means that in step with the idea things just like the net itself may be acutely aware. If that's not strange enough, there's this different argument. There's a far larger system we all know concerning it and it collects and integrates information: the universe itself. At any given time, innumerable amounts of "data" are being integrated all around the universe from atomic collisions to complicated, large-scale chemical reactions all of which might need hugely powerful supercomputers to replicate. Several thinkers and scientists subscribe to the notion that Integrated scientific theory provides a solid scientific grounding for panpsychism.

Quantum Consciousness

Some theorists have created sturdy figurative ideas that attempt to argue for panpsychism concerning the strange phenomena determined in physical science. William Lyncean, a thinker, once said that "one very little monitor will create a little bit of consciousness. additional monitors and higher integration and management create additional and fuller consciousness". He said this once proposing that consciousness might emerge. During this case, William regards "monitoring" and "integration" as basic elements of consciousness in an exceedingly terrible occurrence. There are many ways of framing the quantum-panpsychism argument and one in all the works of this "monitoring" and "integration" definition.

Consider the quantum property known as "entanglement" within which 2 photons which could also be determined to possess correlating polarizations. The polarization of 1-gauge boson has a bearing on the opposite and however way apart, that means that in an exceedingly terrible occurrence, very real sense, every gauge boson is "monitoring" the opposite. It follows then that the "little bit of consciousness" delineated by Lycan might exist at the quantum level whether we discover observance occurring on a tiny scale all over within the universe. What is, perhaps, less clear than how this observance would be unfolded into an integrated network just like the lens mentioned in Integrated scientific theory, this is often one in all the problems panpsychism got to explore in additional analysis.

Non-Emergentism

The last 2 arguments have shown us that consciousness may emerge from integrated informational systems. However, there's another attention-grabbing theory that works with the thought that consciousness might not be absorbing in the least. Non-emergentism, similar to the name's suggestion, is an argument supported by the thought that absorbing properties don't exist. In less complicated words this suggests that the fundamental properties of complicated systems are often reduced to the best elements of these systems still. In different words, nothing comes out of nothing and consciousness should be found in entire systems. However, in their most elementary elements as well: there are particles of this matter. This theory argues consciousness is a universal property of matter and as a result, it may mean consciousness is a gift within the entire material universe.

One in all the foremost intriguing arguments comes from a mixture of non-emergentism and evolution. Several theorists together with the English man of science and thinker William Kingdom Clifford, have argued that evolution could be a method that creates sophisticated systems out of less complicated ones. However, that doesn't bring out "entirely novel" properties like consciousness. Naturally, this suggests that the straightforward elements of biological systems should contain similar properties as we discover within the entire system itself-consciousness.

Taking a fast trip backward through our hereditary timeline might facilitate us to consider this argument in a very additional, crucial means. When does one suppose his/her ancestors develop consciousness?

Let's now talk about the Big Freeze. Many people believe that the concept of entropy began with a sort of bitterness. Steam power was transforming the world, it was towering machines and looming over the bustling citizens of England while in France the landscape was tumultuous as its people grew disillusioned. Then there was this man, Sadi Carnot, who day dreamed of England's collapse. He mused that the understanding of steam power would help him strip England of all its advantages. By doing this, France would be turned into a center of advancements and pride. He was born in a military family and that was responsible for the servitude he had towards his country. He started pouring over the engines, engaging himself with his studies on heat and fire and all the inner workings of steam power during his free time. We all know that heat, fire, and steam power are among mankind's most revolutionary steps in terms of technology. This desire he had in his studies was thought to be a foolish devotion to his country by some while others thought it was admirable and was the need for progression. It is due to this that he became the father of thermodynamics.

You might have heard of the term thermodynamics in the theories of physics but have you ever thought deeply about it? Some of the world's great minds like Albert Einstein, Boris Pavlovich, and Arthur Eddington saw the thermodynamics theory as a certainty and not merely a possibility. The simplest way in which we can define thermodynamics is by saying that thermodynamics is the study of the relationship of all forms of energy in the universe. It creates a connection between almost everything from the smallest swimming microbes to the largest structures that man is knowledgeable of. The biggest exists somewhere amongst the black backdrop of dark space.

The first law of thermodynamics says that they are isolated systems that have a finite, set amount of energy and energy within that system and can never be created nor be destroyed but can only be changed in format. In our case here, the isolated system is our universe and energy within our universe can never appear or disappear of its own accord but can only be transferred to different states. In the case of steam engines, a hot center has its environs to be a colder environment. The temperature difference is the one that lets us harness the energy of heat and turn it to mechanical energy. We use the mechanical energy to power our factories or send our boats slipping out along the silky waters.

If we take the example of a steam engine used by a train, water surrounding the fire will heat up and produce steam which produces pressure that is used to power up the locomotive. Carnot not only understood this but also presented the idea of the perfect engine which uses what is commonly referred to as the Carnot cycle. It is, however, the second law of thermodynamics that describes the nature of entropy which is the eventual unraveling of everything.

Many of us seem as if the universe tends to move towards chaos when it comes to entropy but that is not the complete understanding of what entropy is. It is less philosophical and more statistical in content. In any given system, entropy is a measure of how evenly distributed the energy within that system is. According to the second law of thermodynamics, entropy must always be increasing overall. Entropy can be decreased on small scales for example when you heat a pot of water but on the much larger scales of the universe, energy is becoming more evenly distributed and this is the process that has very high chances of bringing about the death of everything. Realize I didn't say, everyone? Everything includes both the animate and inanimate objects.

If for example, I use a situation which most of us have experienced, if you put a bowl of soup on the dining table, the soup will cool down to room temperature after some time. The concentrated, ordered heat within the bowl will eventually spread out into a more disordered state where the heat has spread throughout the room. This is an example of entropy. This happens because of the building blocks of matter (atoms) as explained to us by Ludwig Boltzmann. If the heat is more in an atom, the atoms will move at a faster rate compared to that with less heat. They then share this energy with their surroundings, transferring it from the soup to the dish to the table and throughout the rest of the room. It is usually possible for a hot object to become hotter but the chances are so small that no one has ever observed that. It is in such cases that the statistical nature of entropy comes into play. The higher entropy is the most likely outcome for a system. Higher entropy means higher disorder because the disorder has a higher chance of occurring.

It is said that disorganized states are more likely to occur compared to organized ones. The number of particles particularly increases in a disorganized state. The chances for energy to be disordered and evenly distributed within a system are higher compared to the energy big concentrated and orderly. Once the energy has been transferred, the process is irreversible like in our case the soup cannot heat up again unless an outside force acts upon it. This is the law that permeates the whole universe. All things with heat and energy are interconnected and this heat and energy continue to disperse throughout the system that is space. This explains why time cannot go backward. For time to go backward, entropy would have to decrease. In this way, the flow of time which normally has no relevance in-laws of motion becomes much more rigid and less malleable than we would wish.

When it comes to microstates and macrostates, the macrostates we observe are usually dependent on microstates since they are predicted by most of its microstates. Macrostates can be defined as the overall properties of a system which include the temperature, volume, and pressure among others. The microstates are the individual particles in the system and their positions and velocities. Most particles usually give a system with more entropy and more thermal equilibrium and therefore those are the systems we will observe.

The more entropy continues to increase in the universe, that is the same rate in which heat will spread to the universe until the system has reached maximum equilibrium. This means that everything will degrade not just sole particles and a swirl of radiation. Has it ever occurred to you that there might come a point in time when Heat Death will occur? According to what we observe and according to the laws of physics, Heat Death might occur in the future.

According to entropy's nature, it defined everything as mortal but because of the unavoidable outcome of the universe's end, it also defines this moment of life and energy and vibrancy as quite a spectacular one because of its rarity and because of its briefness too. It tells us that a time will come when everything will come to a stop but it gives us a solution by providing us with the power to harness the energy and improve technology, build our cities, produce chemical reactions and even better still on an individual level to simply eat, dance and play.

During the early periods, entropy was known as a living force within the earth which we could then extract and use to our advantage. This idea was not correct but it helped people realize everything can live. For humanity to move forward, we have to find new ways through which we can harness this life force. We have made some progress since we started with food then fire and now here, we are, looking at stars so that they can help us understand fusion and its role in our future.

Time and entropy have many things in common. Irreversibility is just one of them. When energy has been dispersed from a material to another, we know that external force is the only thing that can make the material be heated again. Time is irreversible, once a moment is gone, you will never have it again in your life. We might dread time because we cannot stop it or reverse it. We can also dread time because we are not sure what it will bring. However, we should realize that the ongoing ticking of the clock is some sort of relief that tells us the situation we are in. We should not dwell on time and trying to reverse it or do something that we wish we had done, as it will have little of any impact since the situations, we are in are just temporary, they will not last forever. We should also realize that life in itself is much more valuable than the time we are dreading because it is much more than just fleeting.

Chapter 3

The Scale of Everything

There are times when I feel the need to gain some perspective. When this happens, I try to remind myself of where the solar system lies in the overall scheme of things. Sometimes, humanity's knowledge makes me perceive our entire planet as little more than an organic film on the surface of a tiny, muddy planet, which helps us grasp the vastness and wonder of the universe. Have you ever touched something with an algae film on it and felt as if it had been left in the ocean for a day or so? That's us at the scale of the galaxy, just a slimy byproduct with delusions of grandeur.

Do you know that all your accomplishments could be wiped away in the time it takes our solar system to revolve around the galaxy just one time? 250 million years ago one galactic revolution from where we sit, we were in the Triassic-era where dinosaurs who would eventually lead us to the highly successful species of the later eras such as the Velociraptor were just evolving: coordinating their efforts, taking down larger prey unaware of their impending demise. They would live long enough to become the apex predators on the planet during the Jurassic-era, who fought though they had a limited thinking process, most assuredly would have thought, if they could have, there would always be Velociraptors on Earth.

185 million years later in a singular event brought the great dinosaur experiment on Earth to a rapid and relatively permanent end. Something we should all understand is that this is an incredible period for the dinosaurs to have existed. All of human history is still far shorter than even the time from the Triassic-era until the last Triceratops bit the dust in that intervening 185 million years. Humanity has existed for the slow blink of a dinosaur's reptilian eye. 250 million years before that, our planet was in the Cambrian Age and had just evolved into multicellular life.

The knowledge of what we see, understand and presume is always open to new thought, new experimentation, new ways of dealing with our place in the universe, both real and virtual, augmented and in ways as yet unimagined. Nothing we do truly matters at the scale of a galaxy in mind. But we can think about it this way, we can opt to imagine our efforts as the most important thing taking place at that moment since from where we sit, in our current knowledge, there may be no other life in the universe.

In the entirety of this vast thing we call the galaxy, over 100,000 light-years across at its widest, 35,000 light-years at the thickest points, 100-400 billion stars comprise all that we will likely ever hold significant, this island of stars in a fast receding, ever-expanding darkness. It is theoretically possible we may be the only life in our galaxy at the moment. This is a very sad thought to be sure, given our volatile and mercurial natures. It may be that our efforts to be better, more humane, more civilized, more artistic, more magnificent every day, matter more than we realize. These should be made more significant because these acts of kindness, of concern, of brutality, of loneliness, of cruelty, of trust are all built upon the universe.

The very nature of the universe has come together over billions of years to grow from unthinking, unfeeling stuff (if we assume atoms and molecules are truly intelligent) to stuff which has reorganized matter, energy, and the transformation of until it can perceive itself and exactly wonder what the universe is capable of being. We are all made of the things of the universe. The atoms of any element in our bodies that are heavier than carbon could have only been as a result of the violent death of stars in an act of becoming a supernova, an act of destruction and creation.

This is usually in all of us. The very power of destruction and creation in which we are born. Out in the vastness of the universe, we are a sentient slime on the surface of a planet looking out into the darkness and screaming into it. So here we are, alone and terrified. We have invented things to preoccupy us from our fear of existing alone. We engage in them ceaselessly because it keeps us from our understanding of our insignificance. There is something that we all need to know. We are all here in this vast universe, we are all unique since we are here. Being a unique person, you can create a statistical difference in every place you choose to act.

There are many ways in which you can choose to act and stand out.

Say to yourself daily: I am here for fifty to seventy-five years in this universe and I know I can make a difference to someone. There are many things that we can do and have a positive impact on someone. That person needs your help and you should not be in existence if you are adding no value to yourself and others. Giving back to the universe is something that we should all practice. Remember that friend, that stranger, that relative or that person who helped you when you were on your lowest? Be that person to someone else.

You can also say: I am not just a greedy, self-made billionaire who became rich exploiting the labor of my less intelligent, potentially moral coworkers who believed what I said when I told them we were going to change the world but I just wanted to be rich and party my life away, lording control over my fellow Humans. I am fearful of my insignificance and do everything in my power to push that fear away until the cold hand of death claims me. Just saying this to yourself can help a lot. It can help your self-esteem; charity works and much more. Financial status does not make us more or less significant anyway.

We tend to be fearful of life and how we are going to maneuver our ways through it. Be free of that fear. Fear has closed roads for many people. You should change the world because you can, everyone can regardless of who you are, where you are and your age. You should, however, be careful not to demean yourself or devalue the person you are helping when changing someone's life. It is possible. Few people are leading by example but we do not follow and emulate them. It is just that sometimes we are too afraid to let go of our preconceived notions about our space in the universe. You are just an insignificant thing in the universe but we are notions in it too.

Despite being insignificant, the thing that matters most is what we do to serve the other people in the universe. We have seen possibilities if less life on earth, less diversity, less beauty, less significance, less meaning, and less love. This should ring a bell in our minds and tell us that there is a failure to the ambitions of the entire universe. As notions in the universe, it is our responsibility to see to it that such negative things do not come to existence. Helping someone out or being kind to them, providing meaning to their lives, showing them love or even helping them make it in life is one of the things we should aim at.

The moment a good number of us understand this idea, the world will be a better place to live in since there will be a lasting and meaningful difference in the universe. We cannot expect the universe to be changed by a supernatural being or by someone who does not live in this world. After all, we are the recipients of our actions. If your words, your actions, your belief, your compassion, your understanding of each other is the action that validates the existence of our sling film on a planet on the edge of the galaxy trying to see itself, to understand itself, then be it.

Many of us want to make a difference to the world but we cannot because we are in fear. Fear should not be a barrier to being good in the universe. Changing the universe is so simple, you just need to take the first step and try it. Who knows, maybe you will perform the actions the universe is demanding.

Chapter 4

Why Are We Alive

Have you ever asked yourself why are you alive? This question has crossed my mind on several occasions and no answer ever comes up. One of the world's great minds, Albert Einstein, once said: "Science without religion is lame, religion without science is blind.". This statement in itself seems to make sense. Science and religion are co-dependent; none can exist without the other. Some science facts are based on religion and some religious facts are based on science. When all that is said, let's look at the two.

According to religious people, the world has a particular and unique design and so there must have been someone who made it as it is, the creator. Contrary to that, atheists believe that scientists have given us enough information that has explained the existence of the world and so there is no creator. However, science only gives us laws that cannot and have never been explained by anyone. It only tells us laws that have governed reality since the dawn of time. A time may come when you hear one saying, "things are just the way they are".

Scientists only explain the natural occurrences of things at a limited degree. For example, they have told us why a part of the year is cold while the other is extremely hot because seasons exist. We also know why the seasons change, because of the position of the sun in the sky throughout the year. We also know the reason behind us seeing the Sun in the sky, because we revolve around it. We know why the earth revolves around the sun, because of gravity. We know why there is gravity, because of the existence of a graviton particle. But have you ever asked yourself where such a particle came from? Why does it exist? What laws of nature allow it to exist?

Such questions may be answered or remain unanswered but one thing is that the metaphysical aspect has and will always remain a mystery. Who determined these laws? When? Where? Why? Are there other laws that govern their reality? At some point, we realize that science and religion must coexist peacefully. Religion tells us the creator is the person who created these laws. But where did he/she come from? Was he/she created? Was there anyone before his/her existence? Was there nothing? How can we define nothing? How can something come out of nothing? What was there to catalyze this? What laws made all this happen? What or who created these laws? When it comes to this, we can ask ourselves endless questions with no one to answer them for us. There could be an endless number of such questions, one bringing up another, reality upon reality.

When it comes to reality, are we the last? I particularly don't know of any sub-realities and most of us don't so maybe we are the last reality. Also, if given our current technological and biological limitations, perhaps we are the last reality at this particular moment. In the coming future, we might create a small biological or virtual ecosystem that has beings who for all intentions and purposes have a sense of consciousness which is similar to that of humans.

Most of us have used computers and normally what happens when you, for example, write a computer program with a variety of sensors and it sees red, the data tells the program what it can see, red. When some classical music is heard, it translates the sound into data that tells the program it feels calm. When its sensors are submerged in water, it tells the program that it feels cold and wet. These feelings and emotions: seeing color, being calm, feeling cold and feeling wet can be programmed into something as simple as changing the variables. Who are we to say that this program does not exist in its reality, perceiving the world around it in its unique way? Can we say that we are not programmed by ourselves and that the universe around it is nothing but raw data?

Let us think about it in terms of a simple programming language. Imagine a large collection of simple object classes, coded into a massive array within an array, which is again within another array. Each of the elements of the array interacts loosely with the others, able to exchange adjacent indexes while maintaining some degree of structure. Get yourself to now imagine this three-dimensional array as stored in one element of some generic container class. The creator of this code sees a data structure but instead, we see it as a glass of water. Let's say there is another object class, called Human. When a human object comes into contact with a "glass of water", it has thousands and even millions of variables which need to be edited within itself. These include what it sees when the loops defining "sight" are interrupted, what it feels when the conditions defining "touch" are set to true, and what it tastes when the parameters within the "touch" subset "taste" are activated.

All these loops and variables come together and act in harmony to define a human being drinking a glass of water. Now imagine a nearly infinite number of such protocols being coded into a single simulation. The world around us exists as we perceive it. Every particular aspect of this activity is constructed from the neural activity located in our brains. A network of neurons can either be active or dormant, positive charge or negative charge, on or off and 1 or 0 which is the lowest level of computer code. If our brains are compatible with code, is it possible that our brains are just programs written with unfathomable computation power?

Neural activity is based on electrical signals, electricity, which as we know is the very thing that circulates power in a computer. The 1s and 0s tell us when to be happy, when to be sad, when to feel warm, when to be cold, when to see light and when to see darkness. This may or may not be true but our ability to understand or even think about such a concept tells us that it is very much possible. We cannot say this theory is true or false based on what religion has told us. Science in itself cannot prove or disprove the explanation. Instead, all it can tell us is how the code was written and help us know how some variables and objects interact and relate with each other.

Science has never been and will never be able to tell us who wrote the code, the nature of the compiler on which the code was written, the machine on which this compiler was executed, since we are only capable of understanding reality to a degree which the system allows. This is true both metaphorically and even at some point literally. What we should keep in our minds is that science will never know and neither will we. In the grand scheme of things, we are just mere objects interacting with other objects in a manner that has been predetermined by someone or something else.

Everything being said, you should at least know that you are not random, you are not "just here" and you are not without a purpose. Someone or something created a reality so immensely intricate and complex and one of the results was you and it brought you into this universe. In the beginning, a super-class for some single elementary particle was written and this is what evolved to be the first cell. As time and space progressed, millions of sub-classes came into existence. Those that had errors were deleted and those that ran without any failures continued to exist. With each improvement, something new and better was created. The human class was then made one day, the greatest, most advanced and most complex being to date.

Do you know you are the present culmination of the greatest undertaking we will ever have? You have the physical ability to comprehend, look around you, outstretch your hands and examine them, wiggle your fingers, clench them into a fist, stand up, take a step backward, take a step forward, touch the closest object and think about that interaction, think about the laws that made it possible, think they are all just what your brain, a small resting object on your head and interacting with your body, tells you they are. I know you know you can do all this and even much more but have you ever thought about your capabilities?

Now think about another advanced life form with a different brain and with different senses. A life form that when perhaps touches an ice cube feels what we feel when we touch something hot. That when they drink a cup of tea, they taste what we would taste when drinking a glass of juice. Think at that level for the rest of this discussion. When the new life form looks at the Great Pyramids, they see three large silver structures made of metal. When they are presented with a scent of flowers, they see a cloud of blue mist around them. When they look at the night sky, they see streaks of yellow light flowing against a dark blue backdrop. This is because maybe the way they perceive light is very different from the way we perceive it.

We all see the same thing because our brains are compatible with each other. But what happens when you bring a new interface into the existing system? The rules change but the reality does not change and the source code does not change. The parameters defined around a new object's interaction with this reality can be quite diverse. We all see the same things every day but this is an incredibly unique way of observing the universe. We are the only ones who have the privilege of perceiving it in this unique way. The next time you are outside and not in a hurry, look at the people, look at the sky and look at the things we have built by harnessing our understanding of reality. Go ahead and now appreciate them with a fresh mind keeping in mind that whoever or whatever created you had a purpose for your life.

Of course, there are rainy days when everything around you is gloomy and this might make you feel disturbed. However, if you ever suffer and if you ever know pain exists then you will truly appreciate pleasure and happiness. Our minds are designed in such a way.

What happens when we die? It is commonly said that it's not that different from when we were born. When you die, you no longer interact with the reality around you. The state of your variables, your parameters, your genetic information and everything about you can, however, be saved, they can be copied to other objects. There are chances that you could be an exact copy of a previous person, your personality, your nuances, your tastes, your fears and everything about you all in a new body. The only different thing is your memories, the same rules of interaction tested in a new environment with different stimuli.

What is the ultimate goal? The universe in itself is aiming for improvement. It is only logical that the final stage is a perfect being, a God, perhaps one that has never been in existence. A God that could continue with his/her reality and just like before work towards a new, perfect being. Perfect can be taken to mean the best possible outcome but only in the scope of the reality in which it is defined. With each new reality, it can be argued that what is "perfect" becomes better and better than before because each new reality is being created by a being more perfect than the last. With a better reality, there comes a more improved version of "perfect" that can exist in that reality. Hypothetically, there will be no final stage.

A terminal definition of perfect exists in this current reality. However, when we look at all realities at one given time, "perfect" can improve infinitely. There is a goal, and our minds can best define it in one word: happiness. The ultimate goal for most of us is happiness. This is the simple truth that can even transcend barriers of multiple realities. Maybe there was a point when humans were considered perfect during the chain of realities. Who knows, there might even be a time when forms of life were considered perfect. Even a single cell was once the epitome of the evolutionary process in that universe. If we think about it keenly, we might realize that we are all copies of the same human improved upon each new birth.

It is said that God made us in his image and likeness, so perhaps he too is human, existing in his reality where he is the apex life form. By now we all know that we are not perfect and our bodies by themselves are very delicate objects. Before the invention of modern medicine, a single cut could mean death from infection. A perfect human would have developed immunity to diseases, would be invincible to harm and most of all immortal. If you spend some time alone and think about these characteristics you will realize that evolution is not complete.

Have you ever asked yourself why we enjoy high-calorie foods? During our evolution, we had a craving for foods that contained sugars and crabs to survive for a long period. Why do we enjoy being in the presence of our friends? This is because even the subconscious part of us knows that when human interaction is improved, successful societies are built and they can support us as much as we support them. Why do we feel angry, happy or pain? Because our minds are made in such a way that they keep us alive so in the time of danger, we are alert. Why do we build families? Because our minds need to be conditioned to realize that creating a new life is one of the most important goals in our existence. These truths, combined with a multitude of related notions, tell us that we are meant to live.

Everyone feels something, even the most perfect being in the universe. We cannot be numb to the world around us and when that happens, we will not be in existence at that particular moment. The grass is always greener on the other side. Why do most people love fantasy and science fiction? Because the universe is always better in the other reality. Even after dedicating some thought to previously given notions, we can choose to believe anything about the world we live in. Is it real or virtual? Is it coded into a computer or spawned as a controlled ecosystem? Is it run by a God or by an advanced species? Everything we do is meant to make us happy. The meaning of life is to be happy to live and above all to have good intentions to those around us.

Have you ever asked yourself what the purpose of the universe and evolution of life is? What if the advancement of intelligence is the only purpose that the universe has? Charles Darwin might have been wrong, it's not "survival of the fittest", its "survival of the smartest". The search for advanced intelligence is one of our true purposes and contains the answers to most of the questions which we are currently dealing with. The Continuum of Intelligence is a roadmap that can be used for the journey towards advanced intelligence.

This section is meant to help in providing a mechanism or index that can be used to measure the progress of the field of artificial intelligence towards artificial general intelligence, super intelligence and beyond.

There has been a lot of uncertainty of when these milestones will be achieved. This becomes more difficult if the measure of progress towards them is not done. This section does not only provide an index of the continuum of intelligence used to measure our progress to achieve advanced AI but also gives a view on some related topics like consciousness, dreaming and personality. Mathematicians, physicists, neuroscientists, philosophers, and psychologists have been giving us information on these topics but right now, we will discuss it from a computer scientist's perspective.

Almost all meetings and conferences held on AI will require some of us to be involved in a discussion that expects us to define Artificial Intelligence. The reason why this will be required is quite simple, as an industry there is no universally accepted definition of AI. There is the Turing Test but this only provides information on one milestone towards advanced artificial intelligence. It does not give us the definition of intelligence or even tell us what the elements of intelligence are. On one occasion two dozen prominent theorists were asked to define intelligence and they all gave two dozen different definitions. The task is much wider than just the field of Artificial Intelligence. The study of the brain and consciousness with thousands of research papers from the field of psychology and neuroscience still does not have a single universally accepted definition of consciousness.

As time passes by, we are continuing to have more and more intelligent systems and despite this, there is no universally accepted definition of intelligence. This will make things more and more difficult for many reasons one of them being the fact that we will not know the legal and ethical aspects of the systems we build. All along, we have been asking the wrong question. We have been in the quest for a universally acceptable definition of intelligence when that should not be the case. We know that there is a range of intelligent capabilities and due to this, we should be trying to look at defining the range of intelligent behaviors.

The MIT Centers for Brains, Minds, and Machines say that "Understanding intelligence and the brain requires different theories at different levels ranging from the biophysics of single neurons to algorithms and circuits to overall computations and behavior and finally to a theory of learning. In the past few decades, advances have been made in multiple areas from multiple perspectives". This makes us end up with potentially complicated frameworks. These frameworks leverage the different fields of research that describe them. This becomes an impediment to its common use since they are not singularly aligned to the approaches and languages used by those who use and develop machine intelligence.

This section is meant to change and rectify this by the construction of a detailed but simple definition of the different intelligence levels on the journey to superintelligence and the singularity. This new index of intelligence otherwise known as the continuum will have the greatest importance to describe the different types of artificial intelligence and their applications with their systems being designed and built. This index has its aim as helping those who are doing research and those who are developing artificial intelligence algorithms, topologies, and applications. It will help them in describing and giving information on the capabilities of the technique and then make it easier to compare the methods or terms of their abilities.

We have all experienced a moment when we realize that in the course of our life, our plans, preset ambitions, aims and goals which we struggle hard to achieve are of very little value if any. Life is very different compared to our considerations. We all have a final destination and an eternal place which is usually paired with the last aim and the biggest reality of life, death. We cannot pay heed to death since we are just passing our precious seconds, minutes, hours, days, weeks, months, years and decades in living a life that is not ours.

According to the nature of our lives, there is a completely different purpose from the one we are striving to achieve. We were not born to pretend and act as others. Our main purpose is to live and follow our dreams and it needs to be realized. In this journey of life, we are struggling thick and thin to pass and emerge the best in exams, to gain fame and become celebrities and even at times we go to the extent of cheating to gain materialistic belongings. We, however, forget that by doing all this, we are not being loyal to the human being with whom we are competing with. How could we be loyal to ourselves? As we place daggers in someone else's back. We should realize that we are creating our own doom.

Our unimportant fascinations in this alluring world often make us forget our final destination. Death and life after death are real. We have been taught this since we were young children but we normally forget it and leave it behind and start dangling towards our foolishly planned life.

That having awakened in us the harsh fact of life, isn't it still satirical that we are going backwards to our fake, continuous, dogma supporting human-made life?

Chapter 5

A Cosmic Perspective on Life

Am I the only one noticing that the universe is dying? If you have been up to date with everything, this should not come as a shock to you. We have been knowing this for a while. This is not even an urgent issue when you consider that the universe has been in existence for at least 5 billion years and there has been gas in it all along. However, the second law of thermodynamics is still trying to convince us that there is an end which is total cosmic entropy.

This information does not seem to be carrying so much to do with the reason for living, especially the reason why you are living. So, what am I insinuating? Let's get deeper into this and see. So, the question we are asking ourselves is whether life has a purpose in itself. Do human beings have a purpose in this universe? When asked, I will say we all have a purpose. I am unable to tell each one of you what your purpose is in this life. However, this section will shed some limelight that will help you identify your purpose in this dying universe of ours.

How does one discover the purpose of a person or item? An example is a hammer, its purpose is to pound nails. That said, we should know that the purpose of an item requires us to look at what it does. Similarly, to understand the purpose of his life, we have to look at what life does. It can be difficult to get the perspective of an item when you are inside it and looking out to find its work. Looking from outside makes it easier for us to identify the function a hammer performs rather than the hammer looking at itself and wondering what its purpose is.

Unluckily enough, life does not present us with this luxury. We are stuck right in the middle of it as long as we are living. A hammer might not be able to find other hammers that it can observe to relate the functions, likewise, life on this earth is the only life we have seen so far in this universe. We do not have anything to look at and compare the functions with. Due to this reason, we have to try and have a different perspective on life to understand the purpose of life. We have to look at it from the outside to compare it to things that are in our surroundings.

Stars, for example, are in our surroundings, what are their purpose? Just like the hammer, we can find out the purpose of a star by looking at what it does. The work of stars is to fuse hydrogen into heavier elements and therefore their purpose is that they are the universe's heavy element factories. Planets too are in our surroundings. Some of the heavy elements which were produced by ancient stars have fallen into our sun's gravity well and for many years, they have formed the planets in the solar system. Each of the planets has a different mixture of elements and each of them is a constantly changing landscape just like our planet earth.

Earth, as we all know, is the only planet which has done something which is producing life. Maybe a million years to come to another planet will produce life, maybe even moon will. Currently, some moons and their subsurface oceans have probably already started producing life. Each planet has its unique qualities; elements, volume, gravity, orbital distance and much more. Each planet has some greater or lesser chance of producing a replicating molecule of a particular kind and therefore giving rise to life. When given a larger period it seems all planets will make it to the point of producing life. The purpose of the planets is therefore to produce life.

So here we are, back to life, and we currently have a few examples to compare it with. What does life produce? Of course, it produces more life. However, this is not interesting or unique since it could also be said that it is the planet in question that is producing life. If we look at life a little more closely, we see one particularly interesting thing; consciousness. There are many different types of consciousness that have come up from the earth's diverse life forms. Due to the large numbers of stars and solar systems that are there in the universe, the possibilities of some of them producing different forms of life and therefore different forms of consciousness borders on certainty. Life is, therefore, a factory that produces consciousness; we can say that is the purpose of life.

This has answered our question. It might not be satisfying to say that. Like, are you just here to produce consciousness? Like really? That does not even make sense to me. But this realization should suggest to us that our initial question might not have been what we wanted to know. This also raises an interesting question for a potential discussion; is consciousness something we are? Or is it something we do? We should ask ourselves, what is my purpose as a conscious being? To make that easy for us, let us return to our initial discussion of entropy.

When we look up at the dark night sky which is a representation of the tiniest portion in the vast darkness of the entire universe, the idea that entropy is slowly eating away at everything seems sensible. After all, what we see up there is made of mostly nothing and that nothing is spread out over an incomprehensibly enormous amount of space. And yet, sprinkled throughout this darkness, we see those little pinpricks of light we are all familiar with and each of them represents an organized resistance to the slow decay of the surrounding universe.

The stars many of which have planets, some life and some which could have produced consciousness are all pockets of space where something incredible is happening. In the middle of the slow decay of the inverse and apparent contradiction to it, new things are slowly being created. Things like stars, planets, life, and consciousness are all things that are being created slowly. Let's do some math here; if there are planets in the universe and one billion of them have produced life and another one billion of the planets on which life has produced consciousness, there are a million different planets with consciousness on them out there right now, not even counting those that may produce it in the future.

Each of the consciousness is looking out at the universe and asking it questions, learning about entropy and trying to formulate a second thermodynamics law in their equivalent language. The universe in itself might not be a conscious thing but there are things in it which are conscious and maybe as time passes by there will be more and more that will become conscious. So, what might this consciousness conclude as they look at the sky? What purpose might they define for themselves when they look at the stars, planets and other life in their neighborhood, as we have done here? According to me, gravity creates the stars, stars create heavy elements and their gravity captures and creates planets, planets create life and life creates consciousness.

What is the work of all this creation that is in existence? The answer is saving entropy, holding back the encroaching darkness of the night sky. As human beings, we are partners with the stars, planets, life, and consciousness across the universe that are there to create new things, bring new ideas into reality, resist entropy and of course care about our dying universe. Maybe a time will come when one day, there will be one of this million consciousness that will create the idea that will extend the life of our universe just like a doctor does for the patient.

What if all the acts of creation were just made to save the universe? What if music, language, controlled fire, cooking, visual art, tools and simple machines like the wheel clothing, agriculture, domesticated animals, writing, government, religion, justice, sanitation, mathematics, engineering, philosophy, history, fiction, science, journalism, photography, radio, television, computers, internet, smartphones, quantum computing, artificial intelligence, particle accelerators and increasingly powerful telescopes and detectors of all kinds were just steps in a cosmic foot race against entropy? If that is the case, we need everyone's creativity and work.

We require everyone to bring the ideas they have in their heads and make them be a reality. The ideas might be artistic, scientific, philosophical or even spiritual but they can all be realized. This is needed to happen because of two main reasons; one because we can only realize the potential which we have in this universe by continuing with the work of our species and second because the consciousness that does not create is not conscious just like a star that does not burn is not a star. We are all part of one small bubble of order which is in a slowly disintegrating cosmos.

Around us, some people shine dimly in the night sky and of course, they would shine more brightly if it weren't for the large distances between us. As time passes by, these lights will begin to wink out one at its own time, stars will start burning up to their last fuel, planets will be released into space, black holes will consume more of the flesh of the universe before they dissolve into nothingness. Maybe, before the end of everything, the descendants of a certain conscious species which are circling one of such night skies will bring up the idea that will stop it, an idea that will bring an end to entropy, an idea that will reinforce the walls of their bubble of order to such an extent that they will never fall.

A certain peaceful warrior called Dan Milkman once said, "The time is now, the place is here. Be in the present since you cannot do anything that will change the past and the future will never come exactly as you plan or hope for.". Have you ever been to a stage in your life when you feel things are not going to work out as planned? At some point, you wish you had not taken that path and taken another path? Or you wish you had stuck it out at that job or not done something differently?

I have personally experienced this on many different occasions in my life. Do you know that these thoughts show up when we face inner turmoil? Our ego believes that it knows what is best for us and what is bad for us and to what extent it can affect us at times. The naked truth is that the present moment is perfect, you are currently in the perfect place. Beating yourself up and re-examining how things could not have been the same are signs of your ego getting its way through your mind. You decided to use this life path which has led you to where you currently are at the moment and accepting that is the first step towards fulfillment.

A good number of us think that we control our lives by the choices we make while others think that we are just puppets in an important universe and everything has its destiny. When looking at this spiritually, we are told that 65% of our lives are predetermined and 35% is through the actions we do at will. According to me, I believe that some parts of our lives are predestined and we do not know which parts are predetermined or are of free will. A determined destiny can include what family you are born to, the person you will get married to, the illnesses you will go through, major life occurrences you will experience and much more. This makes up the important aspects of a person's life.

On the other hand, free will is being an assistant in the creation process that determines your destiny. Who you are and your beliefs are all free will. Currently, you are where you are supposed to be since the ability to create your future comes up when you decide to forget the past and how the future should be. When you do that, you will be giving a chance for all future possibilities to occur by being present and aware. Your opportunities come as a result of your problems. John Lennon once said, "There is nowhere you can be that isn't where you're meant to be."

For us to awaken our original self, we need to identify with our original nature and free ourselves from distorted thinking and beliefs. These are things that we were taught on our transition journey from adolescence to adulthood. We should stop being resistant to the present moment despite the conditions we are facing currently. This can be compared to that of quicksand which is slowly sinking. We must even go further and try to fight our way out of our impending doom. What happens at the last moment is that we get overcome by the quicksand and we sink deeper until it becomes too late to free ourselves.

Our inner knowing contains all the answers to the questions we have. Have you ever had a chance to experience the sense of inner knowing without evidence to the contrary? This might show up as a thought, an impulse or even an intuition and it just feels right.

We have to use our right brain to make our way out of our self-made prison. The right brain is random, intuitive and holistic. Unlike the left brain which is rational and objective, it does not speak to us. It is in our right brain where we find who we are since it speaks to us through silent whispers. Your life should not be a struggle and your problems are opportunities if only you view them to be so.

Avoid distorted thinking which tells you the world should be in a particular way and thoughts that tell you something, if some people should meet up to your standards and expectations. Accepting things as they are and how they show themselves up should be the right path. You should not accept less than you deserve but I'm just saying that you are the navigator of your life and you can sail in any condition you want to. Leave your shackles and break free from anything that pulls you back.

Chapter 6

Why Do We Die

There are many occasions in which we have been tempted to talk about religion in a way that is against science in the discussions about life, death, and purpose. However, religion and science arc two different things in which one can still find spiritual answers. A question like why we die can be answered by both religion and science. In science, this question is answered concerning the mechanics of life which have their basis on material experience. When it comes to religion, it explains to us in deeper ways by telling us what we do not know, what we cannot know and we, therefore, have to be faithful to believe what it says.

Since the early days, there was a lot we did not know of. Religions presented God in various forms and this explained why things are happening as they are. Christians believed that if God wanted them to know something it was in the Bible and if it was not there, God did not want them to know. As time passed by, people started finding out answers on their own and death was then taken in God's hands. Galileo was among the first people who wanted to figure things out on their own and after some time, he was joined by others and they developed new theories through investigations.

People then started confiding in this approach method to confirm what was written in religious texts though at times it would not be true. According to the approach, death is not God's will but it is partly in terms of the things we can control. Nowadays, there have been discoveries of Penicillin, C-sections, and immunizations which have helped in death prevention. These discoveries were not there in the past and they led to some deaths then. In some cases, people's deaths were preventable. However, for them to be prevented, the practicalities of the reason behind people's death had to be known. Concepts like diseases, trauma development and old age had to be understood. We all by now know that prayer cannot prevent death.

With everything said and done, we all have to die. Why do we die? Religion comfortably answers that. When we look at the Bible, Adam and Eve were given the punishment of death because of committing a sin against God. Being descendants of Adam and Eve, we share their fate. That seems fair, but why do animals like dogs and cats too have to die? Did their ancestors also eat from the doggy tree of knowledge? And trees die because of ageing, what did they do? We can, however, say that God gave impermanence to all things as a punishment for knowledge.

Christians have this judgment day vision and give the "other world" explanations for death. There are very many such religions. The Norse mythology gives those who died well in combat an afterlife in Valhalla with Odin or in Freya's field. According to Greek mythology, the good passed to Elysian Fields. These explanations about the other world give our lives a change from the place we were before, going to a resting place beyond.

Some Buddhism and Hinduism forms have variations on the other world belief. According to them, death is the end of the test and is usually followed by reincarnation. A person's next life has its determinants as the quality of one's acts in this current life. When one goes above the test and rises above preferences, one becomes liberated, finds nirvana and becomes enlightened. The enlightenment is not separate from this world but is freedom from the suffering of this world.

Religions don't, however, explain to us the details of death and life; they don't have to explain to us why the sun sets and why blue light refracts more than red light and therefore making the sunset red. We can agree to physical laws as God's preference if we want. The practical aspects of our material experience follow their own set of rules and they lie where religion leaves. If in any occurrence, experience and religion contradict, then it is up to you to know what's the reason for such a conflict. The option of whether or not to find an answer fully lies upon you and no God worth believing in should reward you for something you never took time to fully understand.

At times, we can rely on our experience to understand the question of why we die and why we live. We are born on the same line of thinking and by that, Galileo's figuring-it-out-ourselves and Alexander Fleming's discovery of penicillin tells us that our experience has a lot to say on such issues.

Science can be considered to be empirical spiritualism since it shares a lot with some of the religions described above. It has restrictions on this material world since it is based on what we can see in this world. It also keeps people alive by providing practical knowledge. Most people experience empirical spiritualism and believe it to be true. Science is a major aspect of this experience. Not even the least bit of it is flawless for all reasons. It is based on a collection of people's experiences who have tried to have their knowledge organized in ways that can help them understand the rules of this material world. It is due to coming together of different people and working together that discoveries like those of penicillin, immunization, DNA structure, splitting an atom and much more came to be known. This offers a great insight into both life and death.

What does the collective knowledge of the material world tell us about death? To start with, it says that we do not die. The cells that brought your emergence have been living for millions of years replicating time and again since life began three billion years ago. You are alive and this means that there are cells everywhere around you. You are a product of the cell divisions and this means you share a common ancestry with everyone in the world since the cell line that brought our emergence has never ceased to exist.

Interestingly enough, since all life forms share a common set of cellular mechanisms, most people believe that we share a common origin with all life forms including bacteria, weeds, meerkats and whales. We are all an immortal life for. The cells we are talking about are germ cells. Germ cells can give rise to individuals and they are different from the cells in the bodies of human beings. The cells found in human beings are called somatic cells. There are however some cells making up the bodies of individual organisms being immortal. An example is Hydra which spends most of its life in water and normally generates its entire body from any portion of its cells. Hydra has been said never to die of old age.

Also, some cancer cells are immortal too. Henrietta Lacks is the origin of one of the most common cell lines which have been reproducing from her cancer cells since she passed away in 1951. Some estimates say that some laboratories have produced more than 20 tons of her HeLa cells since she passed away. Some have even gone to the extent of being flown into space. These cells are responsible for the medical breakthrough in cancer, radiation and toxin exposure. The HeLa cells do not age and there have even been efforts to claim that they are a new species.

If it weren't for the immortal characteristic of our germ cells, we obviously would not be here. However, unlike the germ cells, the somatic cells which are the ones that make up our bodies wither and die after some time just like autumn leaves. Evolution has gone ahead and explained why our somatic cells come to an end. Moreover, the death of all living organisms is explained too by explaining the length of their lifespan. To start with, all organisms including Hydra come to an end because the world is a nasty place to live in; predators gobble stuff up, goats are pushed off the mountainsides by eagles, diseases lay waste to communities and populations and the elements take their toll. Research says that of all wild mice born, around 90% die in their first year due to the cold weather. During the 1600s, 1 out of 100 mothers died during childbirth while nowadays it is around 1 out of 10,000.

Most organisms do not live long enough to meet their death as a result of old age. As a result of this, the cellular mechanisms which have the responsibility to keep them young and reproducing do not have an opportunity to evolve. An example is the mice, most of them do not live beyond their first year after birth and they usually do not have mechanisms that help them deal with cellular stress in their old age. This is the reason why, if mice are put in a cave and protected from predators and other elements, their cells will age very fast after the first few years. Contrary to that, indoor cats have a lifespan of about 15 years. Some organisms like the Galapagos Giant Tortoise can even live up to 100 years.

Death as a result of old-age normally is assumed not to come long after an organism's ancestors would expect to die by other means. This is called the disposable-soma theory. It would be more interesting if it was called the falling-leaves theory since falling leaves are another form of disposable soma. The soma (body) evolved to gather resources and reproduce. This normally occurs even at the cost of long somatic life, since long life cannot be guaranteed in this rough world of ours.

My body would currently not be in existence if my ancestors had not reproduced at the right time to keep our immortal vermicelli dividing. To make everyone easily understand the disposable-soma theory, imagine a world like in the 1976 science fiction film, Logan's Run. According to the film, everyone was killed at around 30 years old. In such a world, there would be no anti-wrinkle cream, pension plans or even elderly care facilities. If someone was lucky enough and had the chance to grow old, they would be bombarded with all types of problems that the society did not have a chance to work out.

Similarly, evolution is just like that. It brings solutions to problems by facing them and producing varieties of solutions. Some of these solutions work and persist to produce even better results. It is due to this reason that evolution cannot adapt organisms to experiences things they have never encountered. The issue of not living long enough makes us end up in another source of our imminent demise called antagonistic pleiotropy.

Antagonistic pleiotropy is the ability of some genes to produce multiple effects which can either be bad or good. An example is Hb-S which is a good gene mutation that makes people have a resistance to malaria but it also makes individuals possess two copies of sickle cell anemia.

Besides, genes can also have good early effects but also have bad later effects. The trade-off between now and later is an ever-present problem for any living system. Have you ever thought of reproducing now since there is a risk of you dying sooner? Annual plants do that. Have you ever thought of taking risks now to win a mate at the cost of damaging your long-term survivability? Most of the young males do this. Should you stay at home tonight and work to increase the future wealth of yourself and your offspring or should you go to the bar to find a companion?

Species that die at an early age for other reasons apart from old age lead to selection for genes favoring earlier reproduction. To help you see this is true, the species would go extinct wasting its resources and keeping its somatic cells alive at the expense of reproducing its germ cells, right? If these genes have bad later effects, evolution is unlikely to experience them and therefore can never select against them.

Mutation Accumulation is another proposed reason for death. This simply means that cells acquire DNA damage over their lifespan. This is proved by the mixture of respect to ageing. However, mutations shorten life. To shorten things, our research in the natural world shows that life spans of organisms are calibrated to keep their germ cells alive and well. The mortality of our somatic bodies is the bargaining chip life uses to comply with that.

Many people find deep spiritual wisdom in the universe from knowing that all of the life forms share a common origin. Many say that even singling out living cells is an arbitrary distinction. Whatever gives rise to us, runs through life, the universe and everything else. Different versions of why we die are different kinds of explanations derived from different ways of thinking about our existence, setting them up against one another is a fool's game.

Dwelling on the past and dreaming of the future should be the last things that come in your mind. Instead, be focused on the present moment. Do not believe anything no matter where you read it and no matter who has said it. You should only believe something if it is following your reasoning and common sense. Death is the truth of life. Thoughts about your death are a great source of inspiration but that will only happen if you let them. These are the words that I remember almost every day.

Have you ever placed sand on your palm and you then watch how it slips through the gaps between your fingers? Very fast, right? That's exactly how time runs out, very fast. One day you will get up with wrinkles on your face and a stick on your bedside which will let you walk a little, a few steps here, a few steps there and in no time you will be breathless. You will no longer be able to climb that mountain you had always dreamt of climbing when you were younger, there will be no time and you will have exhausted all your energy. At old age, you will have only two options; regrets or no regrets. That solely depends on how you spend your life now.

Who amongst us is sure that they will wake up tomorrow? It amazes me how job interviews ask you, where do you see yourself in 5 years? A good percentage of us give answers that are constructed, professional and well crammed. Has it ever crossed your mind that living for the next 5 or 10 years is fictional? It may or may not happen. Climb that mountain before the ultimate end of your existence comes knocking at your door.

Chapter 7

Making A Dent in The Universe

Ever heard of Peter Thiel? He is said to be many things but one which he is not is an adherent of the status quo. When people are asked where his fame came from, most of them say it is a result of his wealth (he is a venture capitalist) or it is a result of his politics (he is a libertarian who leans conservative). However, for those who know him or those who will have looked at him keenly know that those are the very last things about him.

Before deciding on whether to work with people or not, he likes asking people this question, "What important truth do few people agree with you on?" According to him, humans are mimetic creatures who consistently underestimate the power of how our behavior is influenced by outside factors and often to the detriment of seeing the real potential world. Such questions are his way of seeing beyond blind imitation and the obvious, since to him that is where the opportunity lies and that's how the transcend ideology is understood, the rat-race and the constant gnawing.

Do you know it is useless to look around yourself? It is the naked truth that we would all hesitate to acknowledge about ourselves what we can easily pick up in others: almost everything we desire (beyond the core biological impulses) has nothing to do with what we want but with what we have been conditioned to think we should want. Due to our innate character, we all have an inner desire to be social and to thrive in a tribal community, so the chances are that there likely isn't much we can do to completely overcome this influence. It's not a huge surprise, for example, that those around us - friends, family; shape our worldview.

However, there are different angles in which people (especially in their careers and in the formation of their identity) let their surrounding culture influence them and their pursuits. We all know that different people have different genetic configurations and some might want to complete climbing the ladder than play status games in the world compared to others. Some while doing so, pay attention to the minutest details but on most occasions, the reason behind these pursuits dominating our societies is not because that is what people want, it is because that is what they have learned to want.

The issue is indeed less right than it's wrong to strive to do what is embedded in the cultural status quo but more so than often, whatever seems fashionable in this status quo is rarely the path that leads to the real individuality and self-expression, by this, we mean that you never struggle to be the best of yourself. Just as

Thiel says, if you keep on looking at what is around you, you are always adapting to what is around you instead of adapting to what you would become. You should be leading change by being in sync with the world but instead of doing that, you just comfortably get dragged along with whatever is built around you by someone else.

We are all born differently and have different preferences, attributes, abilities, and strengths among others. My strengths and inclinations are not likely to be similar to yours just like my weaknesses are not your weaknesses. I might also not be able to thrive in a particular environment while you can comfortably do that in the same environment. A world that is crazed and mimetic is one where the current status quo drowns the potential of both of our individualities by making mismatched comparisons. You might be good in a certain field but there is only so much you can do by playing the same game as everyone else.

It might not be our intention but on most occasions, we fall to the foundation of what we compare to and it is mostly below what is possible. We are just a bundle of experience which is shaped by our surroundings. However, some links can be used so that the links can be weakened to see to it that no single thing has a very large contribution to where we are leading ourselves.

According to Plato's famous theory of forms, it is said that there are non-physical abstract ideas that capture the ideal form of what is said to be true, what is beautiful, what is just and what is wise better than anything physical in the world. In a certain way, there are ideal forms of archetypes that we can look up to. These forms capture our potential far more holistically than anything we can find by looking around us in a world of competition.

If you are a writer, you should not have your hopes on landing on the NYT bestseller list, instead, you should think outside the box and maybe you should have Tolstoy or Nietzsche as the archetypes which show you how it looks like being committed to something for decades. This should not be done because they are worth copying but because there are chances that you will be their next heir (you might not) but they represent an ideal abstraction which is way more important than the noise. According to them, culture is not living like breathing men but as forms that captured our imagination to help us see the possibilities outside the ordinary.

We all should know by now that you do not have to look up to anything conventionally and significant. Besides, we should make sure that we get our inspirations from the grand and the significant; it is not always about developing an egotistical attachment to what is perfect. The ultimate goal is to see within the horizon something that means something for yourself only, something that makes you strive to be better not for the sake of being compared but because it helps you see the untapped potential which is still there for you to achieve.

Are you still finding your way or you are yet to? During the very first steps into a new world, whether in a career or as we form our identity, we hardly can stay without looking at our surroundings. We need to have a starting point which should not necessarily be the beginning unless we are trying different things which we have been inspired by our surroundings to try. However, there is a point that reaches where a spark of individuality starts to arise; situations where we have a choice. When that happens, do we continue looking around us so that we can play the same game everyone is playing (even if it's not our game to play) or do we find a way to look up to something we would genuinely love?

The difference is between compliance and expression, structure and uncertainty, competition and potential, and our peers and transcendence. It might be a platonic abstract image or an image of God you see when you look up. What you see is a life unlived, a life that is waiting to find form in the real world. Making a dent in the universe has nothing to do with associating your name with something other people admire or signaling your competence relative to those around you.

All of us have dreams. For some of us, we refer to our dreams as our goals while for others their dreams are something that they envy having but they do not put any effort towards achieving them. It is so evident that there is a difference between the two people, one is putting some effort to see their dream come to be even if their efforts might not bear fruits while the other one is just hopeful that things will change one day and they will achieve their dreams.

Taking the first step to achieve your dreams is usually very difficult. Many are usually fixed with the thought that things might not work out. However, one should be convinced that even if it will not work out as expected, the results will still be valuable. What is the first step to take to achieve your dream? First, you should make sure that the word impossible does not exist in your vocabulary. Nothing is impossible. The moment you decide to follow your dreams and achieve them, nothing should be termed as impossible.

Something is said to be impossible because the person who was advising us has never seen someone do or does not know someone who has ever done that particular thing. And of course, it seems easy to tell someone that they cannot do it compared to telling them they can do it and encouraging them to do something which cannot be of any importance to them or us. The moment you think of something as possible, that is the biggest step you have made towards achieving your dream. But there are things which are next to impossible; things like making pigs fly is unrealistic, though might be possible due to the advancement in science and technology nowadays.

When you stop thinking about your dreams in a way that makes you feel what you are doing is fancy, you start viewing your dreams as inevitable. At some point we will all get there, may it be today, next year or even next decade. A time will come when one day we will live the life we have been dreaming of instead of dreaming what it feels like living that life every day.

What happens if you do not take the first step to achieve your dreams? There is a point in my life when I dreamt of having financial freedom, I dreamt of having all the chances I ever wanted, I had dreams to live off my web design business and writing and dreams to help others live off their creative pursuits. Despite all these dreams, I brushed all of them aside because they seemed impossible to me. If I had chosen to view it from a more conventional mindset and thought that I could not achieve what I had been using what is considered normal to them, then you would not be reading this book.

If I left it at that, I would not be able to pursue my dreams, instead, I would have settled for something less. I would have dismissed it as a dream and then made it look fancy and see it as a great way to keep me able to work but that would not make me happy. However, I did not choose that because that would not make me feel as if I am living at all. I would just be living in my dreams or settle down but I would always have that sense of wonder within me.

What would happen if I took the plunge? If I did, all I would be doing is accepting my dreams and viewing them as limitations, that isn't true though. We can do many different things; we can change things and make it better or of better quality. It is because of this belief that we are capable of going beyond what is known that something new has come to existence. The very first thing to do is tell yourself that it is possible. After telling yourself that, make a plan and think of ways that can make your dream come to be a reality. This does not mean that I am putting everything else at stake. No, it means that I create time and effort to achieve my goals. I can be at school, at work and still have time to accomplish my goals.

Some things are treasures to us. I value my education so much that I cannot put it at stake because of my dreams. I have to find how I can manage both and by this, I will have created my backup plan so that in case one fails, I will have another to rely on and live the life I want. You also have to learn things on your own to achieve your dreams. It can also be finding success stories that are the same as yours or the one you want to create. It can also be taking time to learn about what getting to see your dreams come true would be like and how you would get there.

The only thing that matters when it comes to your dreams is turning the idea within you to have a chance to achieve your dreams. You only need to succeed once and it is not written anywhere that you can achieve that in one single trial. Be patient and watch your dreams come to be a reality.

We are currently in the 21st century and it is cool to be nonchalant and stop caring about your goals, to see competition as inherently evil, to think self-help is a charlatan's game and to mock people who want to improve. Anyway, let us call a spade a spade, the world is full of such people today. They will never accept the fact that they are out there in crowds, but deep down they are insecure and would do anything to attain their goals if there was no option of failure. This might be true, maybe, maybe not.

Let us stop focusing on others, let us talk about you. You want to be the king or queen of the universe, right? You want to see just how much juice you can squeeze out of this life. Forget about others and let them bicker about trivialities and stay crabs in a barrel. We are only presented with one life if you want to be the king or queen of this life you should do so unapologetically with no shame or guilt felt. From this point onwards, I'm writing for only those who want to read the message. I will not care about people who are just there making nothing out of their lives and who are not trying to construct reality as they see it. Not even are my slightest feelings telling me to convince anyone about this.

Many of us want to enjoy life to its fullest, explore our creativity to the deepest depths and shape the world around us through pure beliefs and actions. For that to happen, you need to change the way you think, you need to unlearn and relearn your belief systems and start playing your games instead of the ones the society dictates you to play. How do we do that? We all believe that reality exists. We think that we live in an environment that has rules to be followed. That might be true since there is some truth to the idea of concrete reality. An example is where one does not jump off a bridge because the concept of gravity is in existence.

But what about everything else? When you think outside the laws of physics, the reality is way more than what we think it is. The degree to which our perceptions shape reality is more deeply joined than most of us realize. You have personally made a set of rules in which the world works based on the least of possible experiences. For the larger part of your life, you have lived by these rules. Have you ever asked yourself why you accepted these agreements? Maybe you have, maybe not. Most of us check the box because of the fine print of possible belief systems and rules of life we could follow.

If you want to master your mind and reality, that can happen through the process of exploring that extremely large set of possibilities most of us never mind to explore. Have you ever thought of how to make a dent in the universe? If yes, how do you think it is possible? Steve Jobs once said that we are here to put a dent in the universe and if that is not the reason we are living, then we should not be in this universe in the first place. I am not in a position to tell you what your dreams should be. The only thing I am capable of is to tell you is what I think you want and give you the tools that can help you achieve that.

According to my observations, most people only want the effects. The effects do not have to be on the whole world but we want to feel like our life means something to us. What becomes the barrier? Our perceptions which at times are not accurate to come in the way. The fact that we spend most of our lives trapped in petty annoyances gets in the way. We spend a lot of time trying to play a rigged game, the game which we found the society playing and which it taught us. For you to become the king or queen of this universe, for you to become a person who can reconstruct reality to fit your highest aims in life, you have to change the attitude you always have.

You will have to master your mode of thinking. You might at times feel like you do not have a sense of belonging because everything you experience in daily life will contradict the way you think. But why do you have to go through all this? Why do you have to focus on self-improvement at all? When asked this, I will answer in a very controversial manner, you do not have to do all this. You can stop reading this and go think about your life. I always find it hard to convince, all I do is suggest and open some mental doors for you to go in through.

If you are with me at this point, let us go through these doors and talk about the realizations you will be going through as a necessity to make the attitude you should have to live your version of an extraordinary life. Are you ready to face your deepest fear? The deepest fear to us is not that we are not adequate, it is that we are strong and have powers that cannot be measured. It is our light and not our darkness and this is what frightens most of us. You are a dreamer but there are times when you usually have that monologue.

We all know ourselves very well; our deepest fears, our insecurities and much more about ourselves. Are you powerful beyond measure? We can ask ourselves why we are called brilliant, gorgeous, talented and fabulous. We have all the capabilities to be such or to portray such attributes. Is it written anywhere in the book of life that you are virtuous for not getting most out of the talents and skills which you are gifted with? Why are you not letting your light shine as bright as it can?

We have been conditioned to feel guilty for our ambitions, we should not, we should own our ambitions. We are afraid of being the best versions of ourselves, stop, be the best version you can ever be. Is being brilliant frightened? When you get everything in front of you for the taking, you are balancing on the fine line of ultimate success and failure that proves we were never meant to "leap". Some things are worth facing, such is fear.

Your goals are also worth being pursued despite the outcome since there will be a person that comes out after the process. Live in the eye of the storm. If you did not put so much effort into becoming the best version of yourself, then you have to deal with this truth. The world will at times try to knock you off balance. The resistance, inner critic or whatever moniker you want to give it seeks to throw a wrench in your plans daily. I have learned to anticipate it, I have just accepted that life will not always be fair to me and decided to pay the price of admission ages ago.

You know what's the problem, the fact that you don't see the world trying to throw you off. The world in itself whether it throws you off every passing second or not, that is not a problem. Health scares, marital problems, office politics, daily self-doubt, financial woes and all the circumstances that face humans are set to come for you at any time without notifying you. There is a way in which one can develop a healthy sense, paranoia, and give oneself the mental tools to deal with it all. You should not let the future disturb you. If you have to, you will meet it with the same weapons of reason which today arm you against the present.

You have to develop your weapons of reason. Do something to keep yourself grounded; read, meditate, journal or even listen to music. Most of us expect good things to happen and as if that is not shocking enough, they expect them to happen at a very fast speed and think they should come in good numbers. Appreciate the world for what it is and view things from that perspective; it is just a chaotic mess that we all have to navigate with grace. When everyone else is going right, go left.

I have felt like correcting the world around me and the people in it for almost a thousand times. Those in my immediate environment could all use an attitude adjustment. If everyone around me acted the way I wanted them to, life would surely be great and the universe would be a good place to live in. If my circumstances suited me perfectly, life would be great.

Do you have a mission? Two? Three? How many? You are either on the mission or you do not know what the mission is yet. Either way, you need to have control over the world around you if it takes you further away from your mission. When I start thinking about this, I get myself producing the best in all I do. I snap out of my funk and make a realization that all the energy I have spent in vain could be used to make my life better, and this motivated me enough to get me back to work. You might spend all your energy and time trying to coerce the universe so that you can get what you want. That is what most people do, I also do that at times.

On some occasions, we find ourselves spending our time chipping away at our highest aims in life and let the will of the universe become desperate so that we can be happy. People who tend to chip away at their goals usually attract success like a magnet since the work itself is the aim and not the goal. If you spend more time on achieving your purpose in life, you will have very little time left, if any that you will focus on the petty aspects of life which you have no control over.

There is this truth about belief, nobody cares about your goals and dreams. Nobody else believes in them apart from you. There are also times when you won't believe in them too. The moment you start on the path of self-improvement, you will feel excited, you will want to become an evangelist and convince people by telling them how good their lives can be or even you might start sharing your ambitions and ideas with them. How will they react to all this? They will feel like you splashed cold water on them.

A point will come when you will realize that the world is not waiting for you to make your big achievement; to get that promotion, to become the CEO, to top in the exams or even become the best writer. What will you do after that? You have to keep on pushing on, keep working. Build whatever it is that you are building in silence. When people ask you to go out for drinks, decline politely and stay at home and focus on achieving your purpose.

Let the people in the world do whatever they do, while you are winning. When you win, people will come to congratulate you and start saying how lucky you are and that they could tell you would make it. Don't respond. Accept the praise politely and move on to achieving your next goal.

What should goals be according to you? I think goals have to be significant according to me. They help me do many things, they help me keep in check, they give me the drive towards achieving my dream and they can be the ones that make me or break me. The process of setting goals requires one to have put a lot of thought into the process. It may be as easy as writing them down and completing but that does not work at most times, sometimes one needs to go beyond that, one needs methods that are more creative to make oneself accountable and ensure that it will not become something that you give up halfway for.

Goals need to be set with a lot of wisdom. I once did that and it was through that, that it became easy to follow through almost all of them. The first thing is to be specific as much as you can. Setting specific goals has helped me a lot. After setting specific goals, I went further and broke them down to weekly and even daily goals. That helped me to account for everything I did and helped me to consider the logistics of almost everything. It helped me to ask myself questions like, how reasonable is it for me at this stage? Can I make it before this time? It has helped me to make visions on what I'm going after and helped me break it into small manageable chunks and steps which should have been kept in consideration from the very start.

It is by setting specific goals that I have viewed those challenging tasks as doable and manageable. Most of the goals we set are things we are not even aware of if we'll vet to touch them, and is mostly something difficult to accomplish in the current state we are in. Such goals on most occasions just remain to be wishes and dreams. The thing that matters most is the ability to break it down so that it can become manageable. When broken down into small chunks, it also becomes easier to check the progress and how everything is going on. It is only by checking your progress that you know where you are and how you are faring on, whether you are experiencing an upward trend or a downward trend. When you decide to start something, take the first step and go ahead and be careful in everything, chop it all up so that you don't get choked in the process or realize that it is too much for you to achieve.

When setting goals, remember that the first step to achieving it has to start now. The most important thing I realized about goals is that you have to start working on them immediately. That was something that was always in my head in all I did. That is still the word I use when I want to set goals. My goals would not have a deadline for more than a month. There is this time that I did not start working on my goals immediately. My timeframe wasn't at that time, it was not as if I was trying to achieve something. However, the moment I did, I realized that I had to stop thinking of the future tense. I also decided to make it sooner, like a day or two. I didn't do anything that would cover the gaps and so it did not seem like it was attainable. It was not like something that I would achieve at the end of everything but something that I started working on at that time.

Of course, that did not help. I think I underestimated the amount of work or I never got to it and when I did, I just became overwhelmed by every sense of that word. Nowadays, I focus my goals on current days, weeks or months if they deserve such a long period to be achieved. I have never planned further than a month or for some complex goals of two or at most three months. If it takes too long, it is normally too difficult for me to get myself to see it in terms of days. On occasions where I set shorter deadlines, I get the motivation to do something at the moment, every time and this has helped me reassess my own goals. It made me start taking immediate action even the least of things like adding to my to-do list or making a few notes to begin. All you need to do is start doing something right now.

Something I cannot overemphasize when setting goals is knowing your limits. I have been stressing every time but I think I need to be more careful when doing this. I had to make my goals simple and make their time frame a large period. When you know your limits, you get to plan around your limited time and you find everything manageable without being overwhelming. Overwhelming is usually characterized by besides having completed everything, you feel that you've exerted a lot of effort and you are tired and you do not think it is worth the effort you have put in. I have several set goals that have been overwhelming to achieve, trust me it's not a good thing to experience, it is not a good feeling at all. Feeling unchallenged is also not a good feeling. This is manageable though because when you feel that you are working on a goal that is too easy you just go to another one which you think is complex but manageable.

Since you have limits, all you need at times is to know how to push them, not too much but enough that it makes you better but not to the extent that you will feel worn out. Especially when one is done, your concern is to start to the next goal as compared to taking a break then returning to another one. You should occasionally review your progress and see how you are doing. I try to do it every week and come up with strategies that can help me be better than I was before.

Set goals that are achievable and in a realistic time limit. No matter how hard they seem to be, go ahead and pursue them.

Every human in this universe would want to be successful, that is what I think. We want people to look at us and commend us for our success. Reality has a way of disappointing us though, that is not usually the case. When I go to social media, all I see is negativity from page to page. Negativity in the sense of calling others names and attacking people you don't even know. If I told you that you are successful right now, would you believe me? Some would while some would not. Doesn't that sound ridiculous to you? We have become so accustomed to social media, TV and Hollywood force-feed in terms of what it means to be a successful person, we have forgotten what success is. Success can be said to be the accomplishment of an aim or a purpose.

Often, I see articles that are telling people or giving people tips on how to be more successful. How can anyone of us give tips to another person on how to be more successful, when you do not even know their definition of success? This society has warped the way we perceive things. We are all in this journey of life and we interact with people day in day out. Despite the interaction, many of us judge each other both in secret places and publicly. We tell ourselves, "I don't think I should associate myself with him because he is poor" or "She has not yet found out her mission in life". Social norms which are a collective representation of an acceptable individual or group conduct, have taught us what success means when we were young in terms of how and which jobs can make us more successful.

These ideas have been in our minds daily. I went to the web and searched the word 'success' and went to one of the articles that listed 'How 9 incredibly successful people define success'. Do you have an idea of who these 9 people were? They were actors, actresses, CEOs, politicians and a few other famous writers and speakers. There are people I missed in the article; the parents who stay at home, the blue-collar worker or service worker and many more people. Should we define success the same way as these successful people defined it? Such articles are common to see every day. It becomes very different to point out the difference between true success, fame, and fortune.

Something all of you should know is that success is personal. Society has been pushing a notion of success that does not make any sense that we can get in real stuff. No one out there should tell you that you are not so successful or they are more successful than you are, success is personal. I know of many people who are content with what they are doing with their lives and where they are yet some people ask them to be more of that. Pushing another person to be better is not a bad thing since that is what a good support system is but if they are happy with where they are at the moment, why do we think that we should convince them otherwise?

There are people whose goals are just to be a mother, father, others want their family to have food on their tables and clothes on their backs and there are also others who want to be rich and famous. We should not do anything that will discourage such people from attaining their goals. You are successful just by the way you are now. You are the first time mother after years of trying, you are the person taking that first step after an accident, you are the low-level service worker who is struggling tooth and nail to feed their family and even you that rich and famous person, you are successful.

The decision on success lies on you, you set the goals that you want to achieve and never let anyone undermine you and tell you that you should be a step ahead. As long as you have accomplished your goals, that's it, you are successful and that's exactly what the universe wants from you.

About the Author

Craig Gomes

Craig is a multidisciplinary programmer and designer specializing in the intersection of web design, development and branding.

He's a web designer, digital strategist, and entrepreneur with a passion for innovation. As the Founder and CEO of Pixelvise and Co-Founder of Lit Hood, he has spearheaded initiatives to launch and scale products across diverse industries. Lit Hood is a go-to destination for luminous style. From glowing apparel and statement accessories that turn heads day or night, to customizable merchandise and branding solutions that make your brand shine, they illuminate every moment, while Pixelvise has collaborated with over 500 brands, including industry leaders like Dropbox, Amazon, Google, and Marriott, building websites and digital products, reshaping the WordPress landscape and empowering online businesses globally.

www.craiggomes.com

9 789362 697592